This Book
Belongs to...

Rebecca

The BIG BOOK of Mr Badger

Leigh HOBBS

ALLEN&UNWIN

SYDNEY · MELBOURNE · AUCKLAND · LONDON

For Andrea Reece

This bind-up edition of *Mr Badger and the Big Surprise*, *Mr Badger and the Missing Ape*, *Mr Badger and the Difficult Duchess* and *Mr Badger and the Magic Mirror* published by Allen & Unwin in 2015

Allen & Unwin – Australia
83 Alexander Street, Crows Nest NSW 2065, Australia
Phone: (61 2) 8425 0100
Email: info@allenandunwin.com
Web: www.allenandunwin.com

Allen & Unwin – UK
c/o Murdoch Books, Erico House, 93–99 Upper Richmond Road, London SW15 2TG, UK
Phone: (44 20) 8785 5995
Email: info@murdochbooks.co.uk
Web: www.allenandunwin.com
Murdoch Books is a wholly owned division of Allen & Unwin Pty Ltd

A Cataloguing-in-Publication entry is available from
the National Library of Australia www.trove.nla.gov.au
A catalogue record for this book is available from the British Library

ISBN (AUS) 978 1 76011 243 1
ISBN (UK) 978 1 74336 668 4

Cover and text design by Sandra Nobes
Set in 10 pt Cochin by Sandra Nobes
This book was printed in Australia in October 2015 by McPherson's Printing Group

1 3 5 7 9 10 8 6 4 2

leighhobbs.com

Contents

Mr Badger's Beginning

Once upon a time – actually, it was in 2008 – Mr Badger was born.

It happened in Claridge's, one of London's rather grand hotels.

I was smothering a large scone with jam and cream at the time. I was having afternoon tea and my companion was Andrea Reece. Being very much involved with publishing in the UK, she said to me, 'You like England – why don't you write a book about a character who lives here?'

'Of course,' I replied, eyeing a dainty sandwich, and spurred on by a glass of champagne. 'It would be a badger. He'd live with his family in a teapot house, and he'd work in a hotel just like this one.'

And so, with very little fuss, Mr Badger was born, along with Miss Pims, Sir Cecil and Lady Celia Smothers-Carruthers, and of course their dear little granddaughter, Sylvia.

It was as if they had been lurking in my head for years, and all that was needed to let them loose were a few cream cakes, a glass of champagne and a pot of Earl Grey tea.

Mr
Badger
and the
Big Surprise

Mr Badger's house in Mayfair.

CHAPTER 1

Behind the Hedge

Mr Badger lives in Mayfair. However, if you ever find yourself in this part of central London, I wouldn't bother searching for Mr Badger's house. People have walked past it every day for years without even noticing it.

So I shall describe it for you.

Mr Badger's house is quite small and has a thatched roof.

The front door is light blue with a small window and pink-and-cream spotted curtains. On either side of the door are bigger windows which, at night when the inside lights are on, could give the impression that this house has eyes.

Not that you can see them, because Mr Badger's house sits behind a thick hedge that hides it from the busy street.

In the morning, it is usually still dark
when Mr Badger leaves for work.

He takes care to lift the latch of the faded picket gate very quietly, so as not to wake anyone up.

In the evening, it is almost always dark when he arrives home again with a copy of the afternoon paper tucked under his arm.

CHAPTER 2

The Walk to Work

One morning, not so very long ago, Mr Badger set off for work even earlier than usual.

Every day was a busy day for
Mr Badger but this particular day
promised to be busier than most, for
it was a rather special day, in more
ways than one.

On his way to work, Mr Badger
liked looking at all his favourite places –
the interesting old houses, pretty
arcades, art galleries and tea shops that
could be found in this part of London.
He sometimes paused to glance inside
the elegantly lit entrance foyers of
smart flats and hotels, where just about
everyone was still sleeping.

Not everyone was asleep, though.
Other early risers were already at work.
Mrs Mopptop, for instance, was busy
arranging fresh flowers inside the
entrance to Lady Camilla Feather's
very grand home when Mr Badger
passed by. As usual, they gave each
other a friendly wave.

As he neared the Empire Tea Shop,
Mr Badger looked left and right then
crossed the street. He strode up some
big stone steps covered with crimson
carpet. Large brass doors at the top
made a lovely swishing sound as they
were pushed open.

'Good morning, Mr Badger!' said
Harry the doorman.

'Good morning to you, Harry,'
said Mr Badger.

As always, Mr Badger looked absolutely splendid in his pale-blue waistcoat, butter-yellow bow-tie, bright-red tail coat, black pinstriped trousers and very shiny shoes.

He strolled along the corridor beneath the chandeliers towards his office, his paws in their white gloves tucked behind his back.

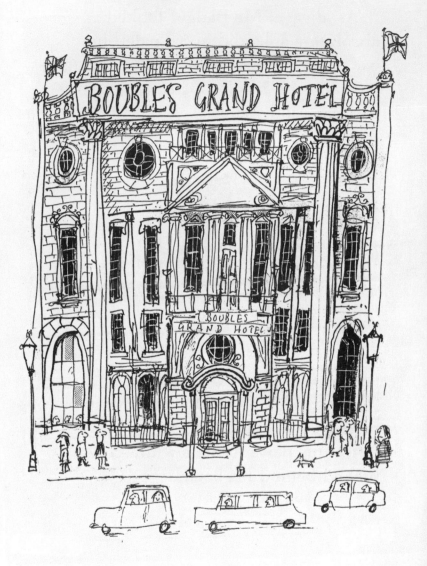

CHAPTER 3

A Busy Day for Mr Badger

Mr Badger is the Special Events Manager at the Boubles Grand Hotel (pronounced *Boublay*). He is in charge of parties, weddings, balls – well, anything really that one might call a special occasion.

Mr Badger has worked there for years. So did his father, and Grandfather Badger before him.

On this particular day, Mr Badger had a very important party to organise. It was a birthday party with hundreds of guests, mountains of food, a little orchestra, party games and a giant birthday cake.

Miss Pims.

Fortunately he didn't have to do all the work himself. Mr Badger had a wonderful helper – a personal assistant called Miss Pims. They had worked together for quite a long time.

Mr Badger and Miss Pims worked well as a team.

'How are we this morning,
Miss Pims?' said Mr Badger.

'Raring to go, Mr Badger,' replied
Miss Pims. 'We certainly have a big day
ahead of us.'

'And don't I know it,' said Mr Badger,
giving his glasses a careful wipe.

Sylvia Smothers-Carruthers was the birthday girl, and she was turning seven.

Her grandparents, Sir Cecil and Lady Celia Smothers-Carruthers, were the owners of the Boubles Grand Hotel. They were hosting the party, and they wanted everything to be perfect for their sweet little Sylvia.

Sir Cecil and Lady Celia Smothers-Carruthers weren't just grandparents, they were grand grandparents.

Sir Cecil and Lady Celia Smothers-Carruthers were rather old and their hearing wasn't nearly as good as it had been. Nor was their eyesight. That might explain why they often didn't notice when their dear little Sylvia was not as nicely behaved as they would have liked.

Sylvia was *very* fussy. She wanted her seventh birthday to be a party that she and her friends would never forget. Sylvia had no idea that her wish was about to come true.

Mr Badger and Miss Pims had carefully calculated what would be required for the party: 410 watercress sandwiches, 820 party pies, 512 butterfly cakes with pink-and-yellow icing, five large tubs of chocolate mousse, two tubs of vanilla ice-cream and six large tubs of strawberry sorbet, seven assorted sponge cakes – not counting the giant birthday cake and the layered sponge fingers – plus

fourteen huge bowls of strawberry jelly with raspberries and cream, and of course the three dozen pineapple tartlets, which were Sylvia's personal favourites.

Sylvia Smothers-Carruthers' closest 205 friends had been invited to the party.

Mr Badger knew from past experience what big appetites little children often have.

Even though Sylvia already had everything money could buy, the invitation had said in great big letters: 'DO NOT FORGET TO BRING A PRESENT!' It also said: 'Do not dress up too much.'

There was a not-so-secret reason for this, which was that Sylvia was planning to wear her best party frock and didn't want anyone else to look better than *she* did.

This was one of the many reasons why Sylvia was known by quite a few of her 205 friends – no, in fact *all* of her friends – as Sylvia Smartypants.

❧ INVITATION ❧

You are invited to a party at...

THE
BOUBLES GRAND HOTEL

to celebrate the seventh birthday of the
wonderful and very special...

Sylvia Smothers – Carruthers

1. DO NOT FORGET
TO BRING A PRESENT !

2. DO NOT DRESS UP TOO MUCH!

Signed... **Sylvia**

Details on back...make sure you look...!

CHAPTER 4

The Guests Arrive

Mr Badger had worked late for weeks and weeks – planning, checking and re-checking all the party details to ensure that Sylvia's special day would run smoothly, without any nasty incidents.

Now, everything was ready in the
Boubles Grand Hotel Ballroom.

The tables were laid and the gleam
of silver knives, forks and spoons on
the pale-pink tablecloths, together with

all the beautiful plates on which were written 'BOUBLES GRAND HOTEL', made a truly wonderful spectacle.

The Boubles Grand Hotel Orchestra had practised 'Happy Birthday' twenty-five or maybe even twenty-six times.

Pretty pink, blue and yellow balloons
hovered in the air, and coloured
streamers dangled from the ornate ceiling.

'I must say, it looks splendid, doesn't
it!' whispered Mr Badger to Miss Pims.

'Stunning,' replied Miss Pims with
a little nod and a big grin.

Mr Badger watched as the guests
arrived. They came up the stairs and
through the swishing doors at the
grand entrance.

Sylvia's guests gazed in amazement
at the high ceilings held up by pink-
and-green marble columns.

And everyone stopped to look
at Algernon, the ancient-looking ape
standing in a glass case in the foyer.
Algernon had lived to a ripe old age.
He had been a close friend of Sir Cecil
Smothers-Carruthers, whose family
had founded the Boubles Grand Hotel
a long time ago. But that's another story.

It was beginning to look like the children had ignored one of Sylvia's important instructions. The girls were all in their finest party frocks, and the boys, too, had gone to a lot of trouble with their appearance.

Of course this was completely understandable. After all, the party *was* in the Boubles Grand Hotel Ballroom.

Every guest was carrying a gift. Some gifts were so large that only a small pair of legs could be seen staggering towards the table set up especially for Sylvia's birthday presents.

Soon 205 little guests and nearly as many parents stood excitedly on either side of a long red carpet, ready to welcome in the birthday girl. All eyes were facing the big double doors at the front of the ballroom, through which, very soon, Sylvia Smothers-Carruthers would be making her great big entrance.

CHAPTER 5

The Big Entrance

Part of Mr Badger's job was to
make announcements at special
occasions, and Sylvia's birthday party
was definitely one of those.

He rang a little bell, cleared his
throat and waited for silence.

'Ladies, gentlemen and birthday
guests all. On behalf of Sir Cecil and
Lady Celia Smothers-Carruthers
and the Boubles Grand Hotel, I wish
to welcome you to the celebration of
Sylvia Smothers-Carruthers' seventh
birthday.'

Mr Badger liked to welcome the hotel guests.

Mr Badger was good at this sort of thing. He'd learnt a lot about making announcements from his father. Actually, his father had taught him almost everything he knew about the Boubles Grand Hotel and how it worked.

With a swish and a flourish, in came
Sylvia Smothers-Carruthers, escorted
by her loving grandparents.

Sylvia made quite an entrance.
She was wearing a very frilly pink
dress with lots of bows and feathers.

Sylvia thought she was special, very special.

It was obvious by the way she walked that Sylvia thought of herself as a little princess.

Suddenly there was a crash and a loud bang. All eyes turned to the back of the ballroom. Someone, no doubt momentarily dazzled by the blinding sparkles in Sylvia's costume, had tripped and knocked over the table laden with Sylvia's birthday presents.

Sylvia was furious.

Of course it was an accident and of course they hadn't meant it, but that made no difference to Sylvia Smothers-Carruthers.

As far as she was concerned, her big birthday entrance was ruined.

Sylvia shrieked and stamped and threw herself on the shiny parquet floor.

She looked a little – in fact, she looked a lot – like a badly behaved tangle of bright-pink fairy floss.

Without any fuss, Mr Badger calmly
motioned to Miss Pims, and in no time
at all everything was back in its place
and Sylvia's presents were once more
carefully arranged on the table ready
for her to open.

The party was about to begin.

CHAPTER 6

Mr Badger
Saves the Day

With a click of his paws,
Mr Badger signalled for the
orchestra to start playing. Soon
the noise of Sylvia's tantrum was
completely drowned out by music,
laughter and merry chatter.

All these happy sounds prompted
Mr Badger to look around the room,
past the guests, until his eyes caught
a reflection – his own – in one of the
many ornate mirrors.

Many years ago he had gazed into
that very same mirror, but the reflection
back then had been of a much younger,
smaller Mr Badger, standing in front
of his father.

Bending down, his father had gently straightened little Mr Badger's bow-tie and helped him to put on his own pair of crisp, white gloves.

Then they had stepped back to check their matching uniforms before trotting off to help serve afternoon tea in the Grand Ballroom.

You see, Mr Badger's father had been Head Waiter at the Boubles Grand Hotel. Sometimes on weekends, and often at holiday time, he would take his boy to work with him. Young Mr Badger had adored spending time with his father.

No wonder Mr Badger loved his job. Every part of the hotel was full of happy memories.

Mr Badger was jolted back to the present by a dreadful commotion.

Sylvia Smothers-Carruthers had leapt up onto the gift table and was ripping open her presents.

Not just with her hands. She was using her teeth as well.

'Good heavens, my dear,' said Lady
Celia Smothers-Carruthers. She leant
over and gently suggested to Sylvia that
it might be nice to read the cards with
their thoughtful birthday wishes first.

Sylvia let out a loud sigh and, curling
her lip, proceeded to pretend to read
all of the cards at once – most of them
upside down or sideways.

It must be said that Sylvia didn't
look very impressed with her gifts.
Rudely, she failed to even try to hide
her disappointment.

Mr Badger was eager for the party to proceed as planned – there was a very full program of games and activities to come. So he quickly removed the mess of paper and ribbons and helped Sylvia down from the table into the arms of her grandparents.

Luckily the orchestra was ready to strike up the first notes for a lively game of musical chairs.

Sadly, this wasn't a great success, for every time the orchestra stopped and there was a mad scramble for the chairs, Sylvia missed out on a seat.

Many a guest was wrestled to the floor when Sylvia insisted that a seat be hers. Unfortunately Sylvia's behaviour got worse rather than better as her party progressed. In the end, Mr Badger followed Sylvia around the ballroom with a spare chair.

CHAPTER 7

The Birthday Girl's Big Moment

Now the most thrilling moment of Sylvia's party had arrived.

Mr Badger clicked his paws once more. The lights dimmed and, after a loud clang from the cymbals and a blast from two trumpets, Miss Pims wheeled in Sylvia's splendid big birthday cake, candles ablaze. It was an extravaganza.

Sylvia had insisted there be a
hundred candles on her cake. Not that
she was turning a hundred years old,
of course – as everyone knew, she was
in fact turning seven. But Sylvia had
wanted a hundred candles on her cake
so that it would look spectacular.

It *certainly* did. As well as the candles,
there were four layers and nine different
types of icing.

In the near dark, ringed with feathers and sparkles, Sylvia's face glowed from the light of the candles as the guests sang 'Happy Birthday'.

Now it was time for Sylvia to blow out the candles and make a wish. The room was absolutely quiet as she climbed onto a cushion on top of a chair, took a deep breath, and…and… and…sneezed!

There was a whoosh of air and a flash of light as a hundred candles went out – all at once. The Boubles Grand Hotel Ballroom was plunged into darkness.

When the lights came back on, Sylvia's guests gasped. The birthday girl's face was covered with black soot from the candles and fairy dust from her fancy frock. Worse still, many of the feathers on Sylvia's dress had been blown off, and those that hadn't were sticking out in all directions.

Sylvia looked a fright.

Poor Sylvia, her cake was all but destroyed. But Mr Badger knew how important it was for the birthday girl to make a wish, so he sent Miss Pims to the kitchen to collect a spare, not-so-grand cake and thereby saved Sylvia's special day.

After she'd made her wish, Sylvia
was led away by Miss Pims to be
cleaned up.

The party had been a great success –
well, certainly one to remember.

Sylvia's guests had all had a
wonderful time. And so in fact had
Sylvia, for she had managed to stay the
centre of attention most of the time.

Sylvia was looking forward to her
eighth birthday party already (and
so were her guests). However, her
grandparents weren't quite so keen.

CHAPTER 8

Goodnight, Mr Badger

It was late by the time Mr Badger had personally farewelled Sir Cecil and Lady Celia Smothers-Carruthers and little Sylvia. Not forgetting her 205 friends and their parents.

Sylvia's presents had been loaded into a Boubles Grand Hotel delivery van and were already on their way to Sylvia's home.

In the ballroom, Mr Badger swung into action. There was a big mess to be

tidied up, not that there was much food
or drink left. In fact, looking around,
Mr Badger realised there was none.

Every last glass of pink lemonade
had been drunk. And every one
of those delicious 410 watercress
sandwiches, 820 party pies, 512
butterfly cakes, seven sponge cakes,
eight tubs of assorted ice-cream,
five tubs of mousse, huge bowls of
strawberry jelly with raspberries and
cream, and layered sponge fingers had
been eaten by Sylvia, her hungry little
friends and their parents.

There was certainly not one
pineapple tartlet to be seen. Sylvia
had hidden these away amongst her
pile of presents right at the beginning
of the party.

What's more, every last piece of
birthday cake had been eaten. All gone
without a trace.

Mr Badger and Miss Pims organised the
clean-up as usual.

The tables were cleared, the beautiful
Boubles cutlery and china plates
washed, dried and stacked away for the
next party or special event. The pretty
pink tablecloths, now covered with
cake and watercress sandwich crumbs
and jelly splodges, had been gathered
up and sent down to the hotel laundry.

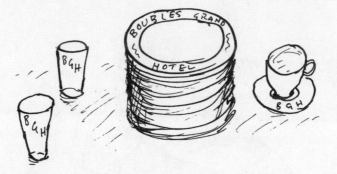

The balloons had long since
disappeared, and all the coloured
streamers had been taken down from
the ceiling.

Miss Pims had gone, and the
ballroom was all quiet and clean, as
if the party had never happened.

Even the members of the Boubles
Grand Hotel Orchestra were now home,
no doubt enjoying a well-earned sleep.

In fact, absolutely nothing remained
of Sylvia Smothers-Carruthers' seventh
birthday party.

'Never mind,' sighed Mr Badger.

It was time for him to go home, too.

CHAPTER 9

Mr Badger's Secret

But tonight was not just any night, and today had not been just any day. For today was Mr Badger's birthday. And now as he gazed about the ballroom, Mr Badger remembered how, long ago, he had spent his own seventh birthday at the Boubles Grand Hotel.

On that day, for a special treat, young Mr Badger had been taken to one of the Boubles Grand Hotel kitchens to watch his grandfather the chef decorate a beautiful big birthday cake, which he had baked especially for his beloved grandson...Mr Badger.

A little later, however, there had been a disaster in the dining room. At a birthday party for another little boy turning seven on that same day, the birthday boy's cake had been knocked off the table and onto the floor.

Mr Badger's father had replaced the ruined cake with his little son's special one. Yes, the very one created by his grandfather. Terrible but true – but Mr Badger's father had had no choice.

This was a memory that had stayed with Mr Badger, ever since he was very small.

On his way home, as Mr Badger walked quietly past a shop window, he noticed the reflection of a tear. It was running down his cheek.

Mr Badger hadn't mentioned
to anyone that it was his birthday.
He was far too proud and professional
and grown-up for that.

However, he had *rather* hoped that
at least one piece of Sylvia Smothers-
Carruthers' birthday cake might have
been left uneaten.

The walk home seemed especially
long that night.

CHAPTER 10

Bravo, Mr Badger

It was freezing cold and nearly midnight by the time Mr Badger lifted the latch, opened the picket gate and walked up the path to his front door.

This had been a special day for Mr Badger.

It was quiet, very quiet, as he
reached for the key. Mr Badger stepped
into a darkened room, fumbling for the
light switch.

But this was not just any night.
Mr Badger was in for a big surprise.

For when he turned on the light, he
saw that the sitting room was full of
balloons and coloured streamers.

Many bright and eager faces were beaming up at him.

Why, there was Mrs Badger, with their darling daughter Berenice, and of course baby Badger, too. Mrs Mopptop, Miss Pims, Harry the doorman – in fact, all of Mr Badger's friends from the Boubles Grand Hotel – were there as well.

What a welcome, thought Mr Badger.

Everyone cheered and cried,
'Surprise!'

And so it was.

Mr Badger's birthday hadn't been
forgotten after all.

On the table lay a stack of plates,
spoons, forks and, best of all, a splendid
big birthday cake with letters in
beautiful pink icing that said: 'Happy
Birthday, Mr Badger!'

'Oh my goodness!' said a most
surprised Mr Badger. In fact, he could
barely speak.

Once again a little tear ran down
his cheek.
   But this time, it was a very happy one.

The End

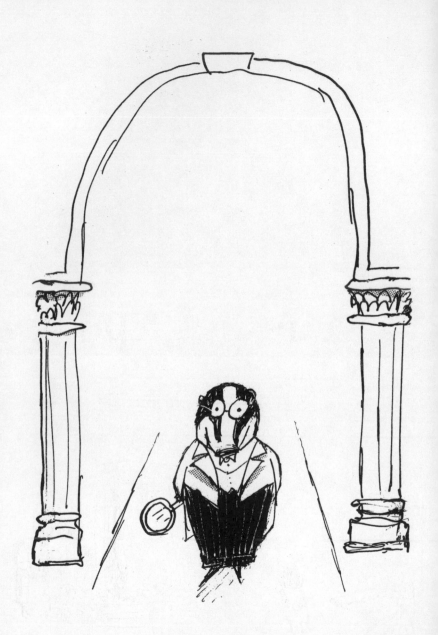

Mr Badger and the Missing Ape

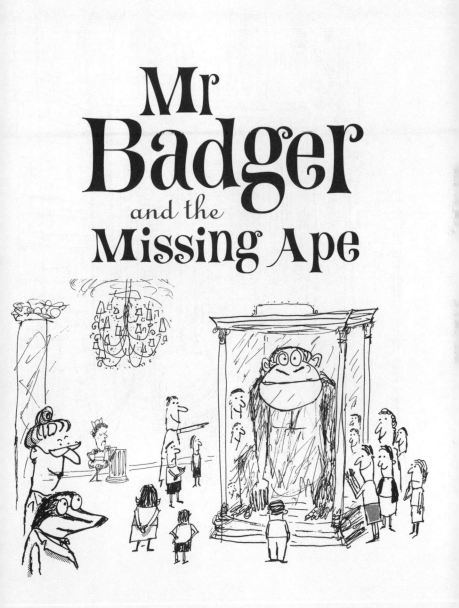

CHAPTER 1

Busy Mr Badger

Mr Badger wasn't *just* the Special Events Manager at the Boubles Grand Hotel (pronounced *Boublay*). Because he had been there for so long and knew everyone, as well as just about every*thing* about the hotel, Mr Badger had all sorts of other important responsibilities. And one of the most important was keeping an eye on Algernon.

Algernon stood in the foyer of the hotel. For years, every morning when Mr Badger arrived at work, he would give Algernon a smile. 'How do you do, Algernon!' he would say as he walked past.

Mr Badger knew better than to expect an answer, of course, as Algernon was an ape. A very big ape. And he stood in a glass case.

Algernon had guarded the Boubles Grand Hotel foyer for years and years. Well, not really guarded; he was just there…peering out from his window on the world as if inspecting everyone who arrived at the hotel.

And maybe he was.

Children absolutely adored him, and whether they came to stay in the Boubles Grand Hotel or were just visiting for morning or afternoon tea, saying hello to Algernon was the first thing that every boy and girl wanted to do.

Sometimes there was such a crowd in the foyer that Mr Badger needed to gently organise the children into a queue, so that everyone got to have their own moment or two with Algernon.

Algernon was extremely popular.

Unfortunately, not every child was well behaved.

Sylvia Smothers-Carruthers would often cause trouble. Sometimes even a scene. Just because her grandparents, Sir Cecil and Lady Celia Smothers-Carruthers, owned the Boubles Grand Hotel, she would often try to push into the line.

Or, worse still, when no one was looking, Sylvia would open the glass door of Algernon's case and give him a kick.

'I tell you, Grandma, that thing poked its tongue out at me!' Sylvia would cry.

'Don't be ridiculous,' Lady Celia would snap. 'It's stuffed. I wish your grandfather would throw it out.'

CHAPTER 2

An Alarming
Disappearance

No one, guest or employee, seemed to remember a time when Algernon *hadn't* been there in the foyer.

This made Mr Badger's discovery early one morning all the more alarming. For when he arrived at the hotel, walked up the stairs and turned to say hello to Algernon, he saw that there *was* no Algernon.

Algernon was…GONE!

Algernon was gone, but where?

At this stage, Miss Pims did not want to ask questions.

It was a dreadful shock. Mr Badger knew that everyone would be upset by Algernon's disappearance. In particular the children. Algernon would have to be found as soon as possible, so Mr Badger began looking straight away.

When his assistant, Miss Pims, arrived at work soon after, she found Mr Badger searching for clues on the floor with a magnifying glass.

'Good morning, Mr Badger,' she said, as if Mr Badger was always on the floor of the foyer peering through his magnifying glass.

'Hello there, Miss Pims,' said Mr Badger. 'I am afraid we have a problem. A serious one. It's Algernon – he's gone!'

Naturally Miss Pims was startled by the news. However, like Mr Badger, she knew better than to panic. She too leapt straight into action.

For a start, she checked Mr Badger's
diary. Obviously he would need to be
completely free of engagements that day
so they could focus on finding Algernon,
the missing ape.

CHAPTER 3

The Big
Disappointment

By mid-morning a small crowd
had gathered in the foyer, and it
was a very sorry sight. Disappointed
children were arriving and forming
a queue, pressing their faces up against
Algernon's empty case and fogging
up the glass.

Algernon was sorely missed.

Mr Badger and Miss Pims decided that the feelings of the Boubles Grand Hotel's little guests and visitors were of the utmost importance. So, after asking everyone to step back, they covered Algernon's big case with a curtain and hung up a sign that said: 'Algernon is away but will be back shortly.'

Better that the children believed Algernon had gone on holiday, thought Mr Badger, than they be upset by the truth, which was that he'd disappeared.

'That leaves us to do the worrying,' whispered Mr Badger to Miss Pims. 'I think we should plan our search.'

During morning tea in the dining room, the most pressing topic of conversation amongst mothers and fathers, grandpas, grandmas and children alike was Algernon: 'Where do you think Algernon has gone for his holiday?' and 'When do you think Algernon will be coming back?' they said.

CHAPTER 4

A Big Mystery

In their tiny office crammed with bookshelves and filing cabinets, piles of notes, diaries, two desks and chairs, not forgetting all the official Boubles Grand Hotel records, Mr Badger and Miss Pims got to work.

Firstly they listed all the places in the hotel where an ape might fit, or could be hidden.

There were endless possibilities as the Boubles Grand Hotel was big and old, with many guest rooms large and small.

As well, there were staircases, attics, a library, cellars, storerooms, cupboards, bathrooms, four kitchens, the Boubles Grand Hotel Ballroom and two dining rooms.

There were also offices, including the one used by Mr Badger and Miss Pims.

'Well, that's *one* place we don't have to search,' said Miss Pims, looking around. 'We'd certainly have noticed if Algernon was hidden in *here*.'

'Yes, well, where should we start?'
said Mr Badger, scratching his furry
head. 'I searched the foyer thoroughly
this morning, before any of the guests
arrived, and didn't find a single clue.'

'How could a big ape just disappear?'
asked Miss Pims. 'Who might have
carried him away and why?'

'And how could they have lifted him
anyway?' said Mr Badger. 'How could
they have moved him out of his glass
case?'

'So many questions and, as yet, no answers,' sighed Miss Pims.

It certainly was a mystery. One which was *completely* baffling Mr Badger. Miss Pims made two lists: one for herself and one for Mr Badger. Miss Pims was to search the main hotel rooms, and Mr Badger the more out-of-the-way places.

CHAPTER 5

The Search

Miss Pims moved from room to room.

She peered behind curtains in the Boubles Grand Hotel Ballroom, then looked for clues beneath tables and sofas in the dining room where morning tea was being served. She even asked some guests if they wouldn't mind lifting their feet.

Miss Pims looked everywhere.

'Just housekeeping,' said Miss Pims, with a smile, every time a guest appeared slightly alarmed as she ticked off her 'rooms inspected' list. Of course, she didn't tell them what she was *really* looking for.

Meanwhile, with his torch and magnifying glass, Mr Badger climbed up stairs, tapped on walls, probed in

dusty storerooms, and opened long-lost doors. He was searching all the hidden, out-of-the-way places he could find.

The Boubles Grand Hotel wasn't just grand ballrooms and marble columns. There were lots of tiny rooms too, easily overlooked and sometimes even boarded up.

The hotel was very large. In fact, there were many parts that Mr Badger hadn't explored for years, parts he had not seen since he was little. At this time, he would follow his father about while he fulfilled his duties as Head Waiter at the Boubles Grand Hotel.

There were rooms full of untouched
Boubles Grand Hotel towels and
tablecloths, and shelves of ancient
Boubles Grand Hotel china jugs and
glass vases. Mr Badger found a pantry
with abandoned pots and pans from the
hotel kitchens and another room full of
nothing but broken clocks.

Alas, nowhere was there any sign of...
Algernon.

CHAPTER 6

The Secret Room

After hours of searching, Mr Badger came across a door with a handwritten sign saying:

'TOP SECRET…DO NOT ENTER.'

Mr Badger opened the door and crept in.

The walls were covered with framed photographs. He looked carefully, his eyes adjusting to the dim light. At first he thought he was seeing things. These were old photographs, of a very young Sir Cecil Smothers-Carruthers.

Sometimes Mr Badger had to ignore instructions.

In fact, they were *all* of Sir Cecil –
well, Sir Cecil was certainly *in* all of
them. They showed Sir Cecil on safari.
Mr Badger could tell this was so, as not
only was Sir Cecil wearing a pith helmet,
but in one photograph he was sitting on
top of an elephant, and in another he
was chasing butterflies with a net. There
were also quite a few of him peering
through binoculars at wild animals in
the distance.

Resting on a shelf were the very
same binoculars and pith helmet which
appeared in the photographs. Next
to them was a pair of hiking boots and
a rucksack. Mr Badger was amazed,
to say the least.

However, he was about to get an
even greater surprise, for on the wall
opposite were yet more photographs.
And these had another familiar face
in them.

Mr Badger moved up close and gasped. Looking back at him was Sir Cecil Smothers-Carruthers, but he wasn't alone. For with him was a slightly smaller, but still instantly recognisable, and even then very big, Algernon.

There they were, sitting in the jungle with a plate of scones and jam between them, sharing a pot of tea and a banana cake. Next to that was a photograph of them shaking hands, laughing and looking at the camera. In another, Algernon was wearing a pith helmet – Sir Cecil's, no doubt.

Mr Badger had always known Sir Cecil was terribly fond of Algernon, even if he was stuffed and standing in a glass case. 'Outrageous!' Sir Cecil would mutter whenever Lady Celia suggested a complete hotel clean-out and major redecoration, starting with the tossing out of Algernon.

'What good is that old ape anyway?'
she would say. 'That flea-bitten beast
in the foyer sends a very poor message
to our guests. It makes them think
that they're staying in a zoo.
As well, it frightens our dear little
granddaughter, Sylvia.'

Sir Cecil would have none of it.
'The ape stays,' he would always say,
'and that is that.'

Now Mr Badger thought he
understood why.

Sir Cecil refused to budge where
Algernon was concerned.

CHAPTER 7

A Clue at Last

It was getting late. The dining rooms were closed and the lights had been dimmed. Visitors had left for home, while upstairs the Boubles Grand Hotel guests were tucked into their comfortable beds, undoubtedly enjoying the hotel's speciality – the famous late-night Boubles Grand Hotel hot chocolate.

Back downstairs in their office,
however, Miss Pims and Mr Badger
were meeting as planned, to discuss
the progress of their search.

'I looked everywhere on my list and
found nothing,' said Miss Pims, a little
downcast.

'I've not found him either,' replied
Mr Badger, choosing his words carefully.
He thought it best to keep the discovery
of the secret room a secret, for the time
being anyway.

Mr Badger was concerned that
Sir Cecil Smothers-Carruthers would
be terribly upset once he knew
Algernon had disappeared. So he
decided he would stay all night and
continue to look for the missing ape.

He suggested to Miss Pims that she
may as well go home.

'No need for us both to go without sleep,' he said with a faint smile. Then he phoned Mrs Badger to explain the situation. Mr Badger didn't want her worrying.

'Yes, my dear, it's a very strange thing, a mysterious disappearance which must be solved as soon as possible. I'll see you tomorrow, and I do indeed have a clean spare uniform.'

He put down the phone and said
goodnight to Miss Pims.

'And goodnight to you too,
Mr Badger. I'm sure we'll find him,
so try not to worry.'

As she left, Miss Pims called
back over her shoulder, 'By the way,
I noticed the floor of Algernon's case
needs repairing.'

CHAPTER 8

A Crack in the Floor

Mr Badger thought he may as well look at Algernon's case straight away.

Once in the foyer, he removed the curtain, opened the glass door and, sure enough, saw a small crack in the wooden floor. It looked easily repairable. Mr Badger was about to turn and leave when he noticed a tiny handle, in a spot usually covered

by Algernon's big left foot. Bending
down, so as to inspect it closely, he
saw that the handle was attached
to a trapdoor.

Carefully, Mr Badger lifted the lid and shone his torch into the darkness. Then he bravely climbed down the steps into a strange part of the Boubles Grand Hotel. Strange because it was certainly a part that *he'd* not known about. At the bottom of the steps, Mr Badger peered along a corridor lit by some lamps hanging from the walls. Near the steps were a few pairs of very large carpet slippers.

As well, there were footprints on the floor. They were big footprints, too big to be human.

Mr Badger studied them with his
torch and magnifying glass. They
looked like they belonged to an ape.
He turned and briskly moved along the
passageway, zigzagging beneath the
Boubles Grand Hotel, along a path that
no guests ever saw.

His torch flashed up and down on
the crumbling paint of the walls and
ceiling. Suddenly the corridor came
to an end in front of two large doors.

There was a little light alongside them,
and a button. It was the entrance to
a lift.

Mr Badger pressed the button and
the doors opened.

Inside the lift there was only one
button and it said 'Top-floor Flat'.

123

CHAPTER 9

Sir Cecil's Secret

The lift made strange cranking and grinding noises as it lurched its way up.

After a shudder and a jolt, it finally stopped, the doors opened, and Mr Badger stepped out. It was dark. Though not *completely* dark, for beneath a door opposite he could see a thin sliver of light.

Mr Badger crept across to the
door, held his breath and silently turned
the handle.

Gently, he pushed the door open,
just a tiny bit.

Just enough to take a peek inside.
What he saw now was truly a big
surprise. With his white gloved paw,
Mr Badger stifled a gasp of amazement.

For inside a very comfortable-looking sitting room with nice furniture and carpets, tables and lamps, sat two figures laughing and chatting, enjoying a cup of tea. In between them, on a table covered with a fresh white cloth, was a plate with scones and jam and cream, what appeared to be the remains of a big banana cake, a teapot and a snakes-and-ladders game in progress. It looked like a tea party. It *was* a tea party, and it appeared that it had been going on all day and all night!

A tea party was in progress.

There was Sir Cecil Smothers-Carruthers and, pouring the tea and about to eat a scone, was Algernon.

They were chatting about their times together in the jungle, reminiscing about how Sir Cecil had brought Algernon back to live in the hotel and how funny it was that Algernon had had to learn to 'stand still, *very* still' in his glass box during the day. It wasn't that difficult for him as apparently he had learnt to sleep with his eyes open when he was a baby.

Hiding behind the door, Mr Badger stood and listened for a long time. Gradually he put two and two together and a very strange story emerged.

Incredible as it may seem, it appeared that this was Algernon's home. Apparently, as soon as it was late and everyone was asleep, Algernon would sneak down through the trapdoor, then up to this, his own special flat on the top floor, and watch TV, cook a meal, or just read and relax.

Sometimes he might have Sir Cecil over for dinner and a game or two of snakes and ladders. That's if Algernon was in the mood to cook.

After a while, Mr Badger checked his watch and then looked at the clock on the wall. It was two minutes before five in the morning, but the clock on the wall had stopped. Not only that, Mr Badger noticed that the hour hand had fallen off and was lying on the floor.

Algernon hadn't really disappeared at all. He was just late for work!

For these two old friends, time had stood still.

CHAPTER 10

A Race against Time

Mr Badger didn't want the children to be disappointed any longer than necessary by Algernon's absence. There was no time to waste.

While Sir Cecil and Algernon
were deep in conversation, Mr Badger
crept into the room, picked up the hour
hand and carefully hooked it back
into place.

As soon as he was out of the room,
the clock struck five times. The noise
was deafening, fortunately covering
up the creaking sounds of the lift
doors opening.

Just before the doors closed,
Mr Badger heard Sir Cecil say, 'Good
heavens! Look at the time, I must be
going. And so must you, old chap.'

So while Algernon cleared away the
plates, gathered up the photographs
and closed the snakes-and-ladders
board, Sir Cecil put on his jacket and
straightened his bow-tie.

Mr Badger scurried along the
secret passageway, climbed the stairs,
opened the trapdoor and crept out of
Algernon's case into the foyer just in the
nick of time.

He heard footsteps coming up
from beneath the floor and quickly
hid behind a marble column. Slowly,
the trapdoor opened. A head and then
a body appeared from the floor of
Algernon's case.

Algernon was back.

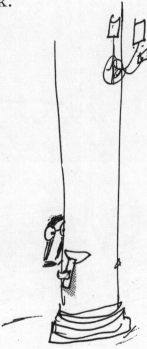

Mr Badger always liked to look his best.

It was morning – too late for
Mr Badger to go home. So, in his office,
he put on a clean uniform and made
a note in his diary. There was a clock
on the top floor that needed a regular
check.

But for now there were other things
to think about. Breakfast was soon to
be served.

CHAPTER 11

A Welcome Return

Mr Badger stowed away the curtain, polished the glass and stood back to admire Algernon's case. How wonderful it looked now that Algernon was back in it!

Just then there was a whisper in Mr Badger's ear.

'Bravo, Mr Badger. How marvellous that our mysterious Algernon has returned from his holiday,' said Miss Pims with a grin, handing Mr Badger a big bunch of flowers.

Later that morning there were
definitely more people in the foyer of
the Boubles Grand Hotel than usual.

This was perfectly understandable, as news of Algernon's return had travelled fast.

And it wasn't just the children who were lined up to see him, eager to ask where he had been for his holiday.

Grown-ups, too – employees and guests – wanted to see for themselves that Algernon was really back. There was such excitement that Mr Badger's crowd-control skills were needed to keep the line orderly.

It wasn't really too much of a surprise, however, that *someone* misbehaved. Sylvia Smothers-Carruthers, arriving for morning tea with her grandmother, pushed into the queue and inspected Algernon, who as usual was standing absolutely still.

Sylvia screwed up her nose and poked her tongue out at the ape in the big glass case.

Quick as a flash, Algernon screwed up his nose and poked out his tongue right back at her.

'That ape poked its tongue out at me!' cried Sylvia, stamping her foot.

'Oh don't be ridiculous,' replied Lady
Celia Smothers-Carruthers, dragging
Sylvia off into the dining room. 'That
thing hasn't moved for fifty years.'

Of course, no one but Mr Badger
knew about Sir Cecil's and Algernon's
secret.

And even they didn't know that he
knew.

Although, strangely, from that day on, when Mr Badger arrived for work in the mornings and greeted Algernon with a hello and a smile – as he had always done – Mr Badger felt sure that he saw Algernon give a little smile back.

And sometimes even a wink.

The End

Mr
Badger
and the
Difficult Duchess

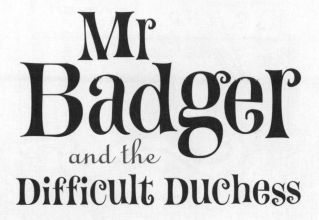

CHAPTER 1

Special Guests

Mr Badger had excellent manners plus a great deal of patience. But you probably knew that already.

This is why he didn't *just* manage special events at the Boubles Grand Hotel (pronounced *Boublay*). Mr Badger was also the Manager of Special Guests – and sometimes *very* special guests.

Special guests weren't treated
all that differently to anyone else. It
was just that film stars and princesses,
kings, queens and famous orchestra
conductors often caused a fuss
because people wanted to stare at
them and point. Or ask them for
their autographs while they ate their
dinner in the Boubles Grand Hotel
Dining Room, or enjoyed afternoon
tea in the lounge.

And one must say that special
guests *were* often quite demanding
when it came to their rooms and
meals, just for a start. Celebrities are
used to being the centre of attention,
so naturally when they stayed at the
Boubles Grand Hotel they expected
a lot of looking after.

Some *extremely* important people
wore disguises in the dining room.
Others preferred to keep out of reach

*Some guests went to a lot of trouble so as not
to be recognised.*

and stay in their rooms, away from
their fans and the staring public. They
were the ones who didn't like being
looked at.

Mr Badger knew this from experience. After all, you couldn't possibly have people interrupting a king or queen to ask for their autograph while they were eating breakfast. Or, worse still, pestering them to pose for a photograph while they were holding a piece of toast or eating cornflakes.

CHAPTER 2

Mr Badger's Diary

Each guest at the Boubles Grand Hotel was important, and every one of them was treated with the utmost courtesy by the staff.

Still, Miss Pims, Mr Badger's helpful assistant, always left a note in Mr Badger's diary if someone special – say a duke, or a famous actor, or the latest celebrity – had reserved a suite at the Boubles Grand Hotel.

On this particular day, Mr Badger arrived for work in the early hours as he always did and opened his diary to study the coming day's events.

Every day there were all manner of things for Mr Badger to do and check and order and look at. And every one of them was carefully noted in his diary by Miss Pims.

Every morning Mr Badger checked his diary.

For instance, today the diary said:
1. Order flowers for the Philatelic Society Annual Dinner to be held tonight in the Grand Ballroom. (Sir Cecil and Lady Celia were the patrons of the stamp-collectors' society. This was the members' chance to meet and swap stamps.)

2. *Clean the chandelier and polish the floors in the Grand Ballroom.*

3. *Wipe Algernon's case.* (As usual, Algernon the ape's case was covered in small marks from the many little hands and noses that pressed against the glass each day. Children adored Algernon.)

Of course, Mr Badger didn't *personally* lower the chandelier and dust the crystal and climb up a ladder to replace the light bulbs, or polish the floors and collect and wash the dishes from the dining room after morning and afternoon tea every day.

Oh no, no, no. There were trained staff who did all of that.

However, Mr Badger *did* give the orders and do the supervising. Every task had to be completed to a very high standard – the Boubles Grand Hotel standard – and it was most important that everything be done without any fuss. Sir Cecil and Lady Celia Smothers-Carruthers, the owners of the Boubles Grand Hotel, insisted on it.

Sir Cecil and Lady Celia Smothers-Carruthers.

'Keep up the good work,' Sir Cecil would say whenever he passed Mr Badger in the corridor.

Anyway, according to Mr Badger's diary, there were no celebrities booked into the Boubles Grand Hotel today. Not even a princess for afternoon tea.

Miss Pims arrived at work to find Mr Badger leaning back in his chair.

'Good morning, Mr Badger!' she said
cheerfully.

'And good morning to you, too,'
replied Mr Badger. 'I've checked your
diary entries and there seems to be
nothing out of the ordinary. I'm looking
forward to concentrating on tonight's
special event. It promises to be quite an
occasion.'

CHAPTER 3

An Unexpected Guest

A telephone call soon after informed Mr Badger that a special guest had arrived after all.

'Mr Badger, sir,' said a trembling voice. 'It's Robert in reception. We have a guest, the Duchess de la Dodo, and she insists on taking the Royal Suite.'

'I don't recall seeing a *duchess* in my diary,' said Mr Badger, looking at Miss Pims, who in turn peered at the open page with 'today' at the top.

'According to this there is definitely no duchess due today,' said Miss Pims, nodding her head and raising her eyebrows.

Now, the Royal Suite was always kept ready in case a foreign monarch came to stay while on an official visit to London.

Occasionally, too, if local royalty dropped in for a late-night supper, Mr Badger would make arrangements for them to stay overnight in the Royal Suite – rather than have them go all the way back to the palace and troubling the guards with unlocking and locking innumerable gates and doors.

That meant, of course, that the lucky prince or princess would then be free to relax, have a bubble bath and enjoy a famous Boubles Grand Hotel hot chocolate before turning in.

Even though they were very busy, and her grace didn't have a reservation, Mr Badger and Miss Pims went downstairs straight away to personally welcome the Duchess de la Dodo. But neither of them was prepared for what was awaiting them at the reception desk.

It was a tall woman. In fact, not just a *tall* woman but an *extremely* tall woman. Her hair was piled up high on her head, which made her look even taller. She was wearing large sunglasses and looked very mysterious.

'Welcome, your grace,' said Mr Badger politely, only just managing to conceal his surprise. To see her face, Mr Badger had to bend his head right back.

The Duchess turned and with a majestic sweep of her arm snarled a haughty, 'How do you do?'

She had no luggage, just a large handbag.

'We have made the Royal Suite available for your grace,' said Mr Badger. 'If there is anything at all extra that you need during your stay, please let us know. How long shall we have the pleasure of your company?'

'Oh, a month or maybe two,' replied the voice from above.

Rather troubling news, thought Mr Badger, polishing his glasses.

'That will be all, my good man,' said the Duchess. Then she reached down and, with a *tap*, *tap*, *tap*, she patted Mr Badger on the head.

CHAPTER 4

A Guest in Distress

Mr Badger was a little concerned. 'Where will the Queen sleep if she drops in one evening and wants to stay overnight?' he said to Miss Pims on the way back to their office, his furry brow furrowing.

But for now Mr Badger put all thoughts of the Duchess aside as he started on his list of things to do. First he had to order the flowers for that evening's extra-special event.

Just then the telephone rang. Once
again, it was Robert from reception.

'I'm terribly sorry, sir, but her grace
is in trouble.'

'Oh dear, we are on our way,' said
Mr Badger. 'I'm afraid our morning
tasks will have to wait, Miss Pims.'

On nearing reception, Mr Badger
and Miss Pims were presented with
a most peculiar sight. For there in
the lift on the left were a pair of legs
and a body that extended up, then
disappeared out of sight. Worryingly,
on the other side of the lift, looking out
from the top, was an upside-down head.

It was her grace, the Duchess de la Dodo. She was stuck firmly in the lift. 'Good heavens,' said Miss Pims, stifling a gasp.

Others may have panicked, but not
Mr Badger. Her grace, the Duchess
de la Dodo, was a guest in distress,
and this was a situation that demanded
a cool head. Mr Badger summoned
the fire brigade, who arrived minus
bells and sirens. Then he instructed
the Boubles Grand Hotel Orchestra
to strike up some jolly music during
morning tea so as to divert attention
away from reception.

'Is this the fire brigade?'

While the other guests were happily
distracted, dancing in the dining room,
the Duchess was carefully unfolded
by the fire fighters and removed from
the lift.

Then she was carted upstairs in
a large sedan chair that Sir Cecil
had found abandoned in France and
Mr Badger kept at the ready for
emergencies.

CHAPTER 5

The Demanding Duchess

No sooner had her grace been safely delivered to the Royal Suite than Mr Badger, deep in discussion with the florist, was notified that there was another call from reception.

'Her grace has complained that the bed is too short,' said Robert.

Mr Badger, never one to get flustered, made his way up, up, up to the top floor and tapped on the door.

'*Entrez*,' said a frosty voice. Fortunately Mr Badger knew a little French, and so he entered the room.

The Duchess was resting, her extra-long legs hanging over and off the end of the bed.

'Well, your grace, this just won't do,' said Mr Badger with considerable aplomb.

'My thoughts exactly,' responded the long figure grumpily, as she slurped on a milkshake.

Mr Badger picked up the telephone
and made a quick call.

Within minutes, a cluster of Boubles
Grand Hotel handymen were at the
door of the Royal Suite, carrying
a bed.

Once inside – and only then with the
Duchess's permission, of course – they
lifted her amazingly straight legs and

'Gently now, chaps,' said Mr Badger.

(under Mr Badger's supervision) slid
the extra bed in beneath her dainty feet.

The Duchess didn't need to lift a
finger.

'Wonderful,' said Mr Badger. 'Thank you, gentlemen.'

There were no thanks from the Duchess de la Dodo, though. She was busy gulping down chocolates, having finished her milkshake.

CHAPTER 6

The Special Guest's Requests

With the Duchess's comfort ensured, Mr Badger returned downstairs. He needed to oversee the re-hanging of the recently cleaned Boubles Grand Hotel Ballroom chandelier and inspect the splendidly re-polished parquetry floor. It was so shiny that Miss Pims and Mr Badger could see their faces reflected in it.

Thanks to Miss Pims' planning and Mr Badger's expert organising skills, preparations for the stamp-collectors' dinner were under control and running smoothly.

Unfortunately, the atmosphere in the hotel kitchen was far from relaxed.

Those in charge of room service, and in turn the kitchen staff, were finding it difficult to keep up with a flood of requests. And every request came from the special guest in the Royal Suite.

For example, the Duchess had ordered: imported Belgian chocolate-chip ice-cream; a Scottish sponge cake, which had to be flown all the way down from Edinburgh by helicopter; and lots of lime-flavoured Latvian lemonade – all to be supplied 'on the double'.

And, everything was demanded and received without a single 'please' or 'thank you'.

Up and down, up and down stairways and into lifts staggered the Boubles Grand Hotel staff with a seemingly endless procession of sweets and treats.

The Duchess even sent a bellboy out for pizzas!

'I'll attend to it immediately, sir,' said Mr Badger to a disgruntled guest who complained that the Boubles Grand Hotel smelt like a pizza parlour.

It seemed to some that the hotel was looking after just one guest.

It wasn't only food that the Duchess de la Dodo was ordering, either. She demanded many toys and games be delivered to her room quick smart – not to mention three television sets for her suite. Apparently there were three programs on at the same time on different channels, and she didn't want to miss a thing.

'I must admit her grace *is* a rather demanding guest,' said Mr Badger to Miss Pims after supervising the installation of the third television.

'Hmm, to say the least,' came the reply.

The Duchess was making the most of her stay at the Boubles Grand Hotel.

CHAPTER 7

Stamps Galore

By now it was late afternoon and the Boubles Grand Hotel foyer was filling with eager stamp-collectors carrying their collections.

Some philatelists swapped stories in the foyer.

They were a rather shy lot, though
this had never stopped them from
having a wonderful – if quiet – time
at their annual get-together. It was a
chance to see each other's stamps and
maybe to do some serious swapping.
For many, this was the one evening
in the year when their most precious
stamps were revealed to other collectors.

Mr Badger and Miss Pims watched as guests streamed through the foyer into the Boubles Grand Hotel Ballroom. Mr Badger quietly gave instructions, greeted people, checked name cards and places, and made sure guests were shown to their correct tables. Most importantly, he did his best to make everyone feel welcome.

Philatelists were filling the foyer.

Sir Cecil was always ready for a chat.

'Good evening, Sir Cecil – and
how are we tonight, Lady Celia?'
said Mr Badger as the Smothers-
Carrutherses were escorted to their
VIP table. It was a well-kept secret,
but Sir Cecil and Lady Celia weren't
interested in stamps at all; nonetheless,
they were honoured to be patrons, and
never missed a dinner. Especially as the
Boubles Grand Hotel was like a second
home to the Philatelic Society.

Upstairs in the Royal Suite, the Duchess had also been very busy. She'd insisted on ordering every last luxury that the hotel could offer, all the while never once removing her dark glasses.

Meanwhile, downstairs, the kitchen was still on red alert, as her grace hadn't stopped eating since she'd arrived.

Now, though, with the sun going down and the lights outside going on, the Duchess was getting bored in her Royal Suite.

There was nothing of interest on any of the televisions, so her grace made yet another call to room service.

'Send up the bellboys with my sedan chair,' she said. 'I wish to go downstairs.'

CHAPTER 8

An Unexpected Entrance

In the Boubles Grand Hotel Ballroom, a speech had been made by the President of the Philatelic Society and the stamp-collectors were enjoying their dinner, exchanging sensational stamp stories and swapping feverishly. Mr Badger had turned the air-conditioning off so as not to cause the guests discomfort, just in case the breeze ruffled the pages of their precious albums and unhinged the contents.

Suddenly, a hush fell upon the
room and all eyes turned towards an
extraordinarily tall figure with a curled
lip wearing sunglasses standing at the
doorway. The Duchess had arrived,
unannounced. She was on the lookout
for some excitement.

'Who *is* that?' said Lady Celia to
Mr Badger, who had just brought her
a special cup of tea.

'Her grace, the Duchess de la Dodo,'
replied Mr Badger.

'Never heard of her,' snapped Lady
Celia as she squinted at the Duchess,
adjusting her glasses. 'I can't put my
finger on it, but there *is* something
familiar about her. Dreadful manners,
I must say, wearing sunglasses indoors.
A very nice fur she is wearing, though –
it reminds me of one I used to wear.
Hmmm, and the shoes, too.'

Mr Badger and Miss Pims watched as the Duchess, spotting an uneaten raspberry-meringue pie with pineapple coulis, set off towards the sweets trolley.

Clomp, clomp, clomp went her feet as she strode into the room. Despite those long, long legs, Mr Badger noticed that the Duchess did not move very gracefully.

If it hadn't have been for Mr Badger's quick thinking, what happened next would have made the morning newspapers, if not the *International Philatelic News*. For, with a dreadful squeak and then a shriek, the Duchess de la Dodo slipped on the beautifully re-polished Boubles Grand Hotel Ballroom floor.

Gasping in astonishment, the stamp-collectors looked up as the Duchess became airborne, her extra-long legs flailing above their heads. Her arms flapped about like a great big bird, fanning hats off heads and menus off tables. Most distressing of all, stamps flew everywhere as she struggled to steady herself.

The guests were momentarily stunned
into silence. Then the crowd screamed
as one as the Duchess – who they only
knew as a very tall woman – lurched
back mid-air, right into the newly
restored Boubles Grand Hotel chandelier.

'Looks like an attention-seeker,' said Lady Celia.

Back and forth she swayed,
suspended by her magnificent hair like
a great gangly spider. It was a truly
horrifying spectacle. Everyone clutched
their seats, as thousands of precious
stamps fluttered about the Boubles
Grand Hotel Ballroom.

Then, bit by bit, the Duchess –
literally – began to fall apart.

First one long leg, and then another,
dropped to the floor with a loud,
echoing *thud*. Moans filled the room as,
straight after that dreadful scene, the
Duchess's head and hair separated, her
sunglasses flew off and she plunged
to the floor with a crash, right in
front of Sir Cecil and Lady Smothers-
Carruthers. Her grace's hair, though,
was left hanging in the chandelier.

'Good heavens! I *thought* she reminded me of someone!' said Lady Celia, breaking a shocked silence.

'Remarkable,' mumbled Sir Cecil, scratching his head.

For, lying on the floor at their feet, surrounded by stamps, was their darling little granddaughter, Sylvia Smothers-Carruthers.

Mr Badger, sensing that the reputation of the Boubles Grand Hotel was at stake, stepped forward and applauded enthusiastically. 'BRAVO!' he cried.

Following Mr Badger's lead, the whole Philatelic Society joined in with thunderous applause, believing that this performance had all been part of the evening's entertainment, compliments of Sir Cecil and Lady Celia – sort of a spectacular stamp mix-and-match.

Lady Celia was not amused.

Mr Badger's quick thinking had saved little Sylvia – in fact the whole Smothers-Carruthers family – from a dreadful embarrassment.

'She's training to be in a circus,' said Lady Celia with a tense smile to some very important stamp-collectors at the next table. 'Isn't she talented?'

CHAPTER 9

A Stamp of Approval

'You have quite a bit of explaining to do, young lady,' said Lady Celia to a surly Sylvia. 'How did you get your hands on my fur? Not to mention my shoes and my glasses!'

Lady Celia was painfully aware of Sylvia's constant attention-seeking, and it was true that Sylvia desired to be a circus acrobat. 'A clown is more like it,' Lady Celia would hurrumph. 'There'll be no acrobats in this family.'

Mr Badger felt it best not to say anything about Sylvia's occupation of the Royal Suite, not even the three television sets, the food, the drinks or the pizzas, and *especially* not the cake flown down from Edinburgh.

Someone was a naughty girl.

Sylvia was in enough trouble as it was, and he did not wish to cause Sir Cecil or Lady Celia any more anxiety.

'Come and sit!' demanded Lady Celia, one hand pointing at the empty seat

next to her and the other at her very
grumpy granddaughter. 'And take off
those earrings.'

While Mr Badger quietly directed
staff to gather up Sylvia's stilts, retrieve
her big wig from the chandelier and
collect her extra-long frock extension
from the floor, Sylvia made herself
comfortable and looked over the
Philatelic Society's special menu,
as if nothing out of the ordinary had
taken place.

Sylvia joined Lady Celia for dessert.

'You've missed the main course, but
you may order dessert,' Lady Celia
snapped. 'I'm sure the kitchen would be
more than happy to prepare something
very special for you.'

Down below, deep in the Boubles Grand Hotel kitchen, the red-alert light flashed on once again.

Meanwhile, the stamp-collectors were in a state of extreme excitement. Never before had a stamp-swapping evening been as thrilling, resulting in so many unexpected discoveries.

An extreme excitement of stamp-collectors.

'Well done, Mr Badger,' whispered
a grateful Sir Cecil with a wink.

'Happy to be of service, sir.'

Mr Badger took the evening's events
in his stride. After all, he *was* the
Boubles Grand Hotel's Special Events
Manager – and this had certainly been
a special event. In fact, the whole day
had been special. Mr Badger had a
feeling that the kitchen staff would
agree.

CHAPTER 10

A Cup of Cocoa
and a Chat

Much later, after Sylvia Smothers-Carruthers had been safely deposited home and tucked into her very own bed, and the Royal Suite had been cleared of pizza boxes, comic books and the three televisions, Mr Badger went home; his work, for today at least, was done.

The Boubles Grand Hotel Royal Suite was ready once more for a royal visitor – hopefully a real one next time.

By the time Mr Badger arrived home,
baby Badger and darling daughter
Berenice were fast asleep. But not
so Mrs Badger.

She was waiting up with hot cocoa
and sandwiches to share with her
husband.

Mrs Badger was eager to hear about
the day's events. And it must be said
that Mr Badger took a great delight
in relating them to her, for it was not
every day that the Philatelic Society
Annual Dinner featured a guest as
memorable as the Duchess de la Dodo.

A little later, just before he closed his eyes and fell asleep, Mr Badger smiled as he wondered just what he would find in his diary tomorrow morning at the Boubles Grand Hotel.

The End

Mr Badger

and the

Magic Mirror

CHAPTER 1

A Bedtime Story

Whenever Mr Badger came home tired after a hard day's work at the Boubles Grand Hotel, Mrs Badger understood why – for every day brought with it new adventures. Mrs Badger looked forward to hearing all about them at dinnertime.

No matter how exhausted Mr Badger might be, he always made sure he read a bedtime story to his darling daughter Berenice, and baby Badger, too. If Mr Badger dozed off in the middle of a story, Mrs Badger knew better than to rouse him from his early evening snooze.

On this particularly wintry evening, though, it was going to take an extra-special effort for Mr Badger to sit and read a story, for he felt absolutely worn out. His day at the Boubles Grand Hotel had been even more eventful than usual.

Still, the last thing he wanted was
to disappoint the little badgers waiting
patiently for him. So, Mr Badger made
himself comfortable in the special reading
chair next to their beds and began.

'Once upon a time…' said Mr Badger,
as two small, eager faces peered up
at him. He knew this part by heart, for
every story seemed to begin this way.
'Once upon a time, there was…'

As he was reading, Mr Badger thought about his day. And what a strange day it had been – surely as strange as any story in the book he was holding between his paws...

CHAPTER 2

Tea and Toast

Mr Badger's day had begun normally enough. After tea and toast, he had kissed Mrs Badger, darling daughter Berenice, and baby Badger, too. Then he had walked to work at the Boubles Grand Hotel while the moon was still high in the chilly sky.

'Good morning, Algernon,' said
Mr Badger with a wave of his arm
as he passed the big ape standing
in the glass case in the foyer.

Mr Badger always greeted Algernon.

Continuing along the corridor,
Mr Badger noticed loud hammering
sounds coming from the top of the
stairs. Workmen were busy attaching
a large mirror with a golden frame onto
the wall at the top of the main staircase.
Mr Badger recalled that Sir Cecil
Smothers-Carruthers had requested
a mirror be moved from one of his
private rooms and hung above the
stairs. He made a little note to himself
to check on its progress later.

Once in his office, there was the
diary to be checked and mail to be read.
A postcard from Miss Pims, Mr Badger's
assistant, had arrived from Spain.
'Having a lovely holiday in the sun.
Back soon,' it said.

It was a postcard, from Miss Pims.

Lucky Miss Pims, thought Mr Badger.
For a moment, he imagined how nice
it would be to escape the cold London
winter. Not that he thought about it for
very long. He had things to do.

CHAPTER 3

Things to Do

First of all, Mr Badger had to make sure that everything in the hotel was spick and span. That meant fires lit to keep the rooms warm and cosy; fresh flowers arranged nicely in vases; pictures hung straight on walls; cushions fluffed up on sofas in the hotel foyer; and the starched tablecloths and pale-pink napkins folded and laid on tables in the dining room, ready for morning tea.

Mr Badger wanted a closer look.

Most importantly, Mr Badger needed
to see how the new mirror was looking.
He proceeded up the stairs, noting that
the workmen had gone and Sir Cecil's
mirror was now in place. He paused
for a moment. It looked splendid.
Mr Badger had thought he knew every
single piece of furniture in the hotel, but
he had never seen *this* mirror before.

'Hmm,' he said, studying the mirror so closely that the end of his nose brushed against the glass and left a little smudge.

The image in the mirror looked foggy and unclear. Was it because of the mirror's age? Or was it Mr Badger's warm breath on the cold surface?

Mr Badger straightened his bow-tie and adjusted his vest and scarlet coat.

It was certainly not an ordinary mirror.

He couldn't quite put his finger on it, but there was something odd about this mirror.

He reached for a nearby chair and, dusting the soles of his shoes, carefully climbed onto the seat. Then he gently touched the surface of the mirror with his white-gloved paws.

'Remarkable!' Mr Badger said softly to himself.

He looked around; there was no one in sight. Who knows what made Mr Badger do what he did next? Even he couldn't have explained it if you'd asked – but, extending a foot, he stepped off the chair and leapt...right in through the mirror.

CHAPTER 4

Mr Badger, Explorer

What a thrilling *discovery*, thought Mr Badger as he felt a delicious warm breeze on the other side of the mirror.

As a little badger, he had read about magic mirrors in books. And that's where he believed they belonged. Well, that was where he *had* believed they belonged, until now.

Mr Badger had never expected to discover one at the Boubles Grand Hotel! Let alone be able to climb into or actually *through* one.

Now in front of him was an astonishing sight. Tall pink columns shaped like palm trees reached up to a ceiling that looked like the sky.

Mr Badger thought it was incredible.

Directly in front of Mr Badger was an enormous castle surrounded by a moat. Long coloured flags fluttered from towers popping up above the battlements. At the very top was a huge slide that curled around and around, then disappeared down into the castle through the roof. Nearby was a beach with clear yellow sand. And on the beach sat a bright tin bucket and spade, next to a small sandcastle. Mr Badger could see a trail of footprints going back and forth from the sandcastle to the big castle. There were extra-big footprints mixed in with the smaller ones.

Mr Badger cupped his ear and listened to the gentle sound of waves splashing against the shore.

How marvellous! Fancy finding a place like this. Better still, to find it right here in the Boubles Grand Hotel!

He could hardly wait to show Miss Pims when she arrived back from her holiday – and what a place to bring Berenice, baby Badger and Mrs Badger, too!

Now, though, it was time for Mr Badger to do some exploring on his own.

CHAPTER 5

Strange Reflections

Meanwhile, back on the other side of the mirror, Lady Celia Smothers-Carruthers had arrived for morning tea with Sylvia, her beloved little granddaughter.

'Oh, do hurry up. Must you dawdle so?' snapped Lady Celia.

Sylvia Smothers-Carruthers was always on the lookout for something naughty to get up to — be it someone to tease or trip, a table to overturn, maybe even a dainty dish to drop with a crash. The louder the clatter, or the more the mess, the better.

'Anything for attention,' her grandmother would often say with an exasperated sigh.

Sylvia soon spotted the mirror and leapt up the stairs, two at a time. As she reached the top she gave a shriek of delight – for on the other side of the mirror, through the glass, she could see Mr Badger!

Sylvia could see something, but not so Lady Celia.

Sylvia Smothers-Carruthers never liked to miss out on anything, so she called her grandmother, pointed at the mirror and demanded that they go in and join him.

'Sylvia, dear, don't be ridiculous,' said Lady Celia, rolling her eyes and shaking her walking stick. 'Go in and join *whom*? I see nothing but our reflections – and even they are unclear. It's like looking at oneself in a fog. What a stupid old mirror. It should be thrown out. Why *does* your grandfather keep such rubbish around the hotel?

'Anyway, an Australian tour group is expected today for morning tea, so there'll probably be a stampede for the scones in the dining room.'

Lady Celia stomped off, expecting Sylvia to follow. But Sylvia had other plans.

She waited for her grandmother to reach the bottom of the stairs. Once Lady Celia had entered the dining room, Sylvia put a cushion on the chair that was standing in front of the mirror and climbed up.

Sylvia usually did what she wanted.

She peered into the mirror, touched the surface and then, with a small silent jump, dived in.

Lady Celia was huffing loudly to herself in the dining room. 'Where has that silly girl gone to now?' she said through gritted teeth. 'If the Australians eat all the scones and I miss out, there'll be *real* trouble.'

She stomped back up the stairs, looking this way and that. 'Oh, where is she?' her ladyship said, looking very glum indeed.

Lady Celia was getting cross.

Being a trifle deaf, she didn't hear the tap-tap-tapping of small fingers. And as her back was now to the mirror, she didn't see the waving hand and the tip of a bow behind her, on the other side of the glass.

'What's *this* doing here?' said Lady
Celia, almost stumbling over the chair
with the cushion on top. If she'd been
wearing her glasses, and had taken
the time to look closely at the cushion,
Lady Celia may well have noticed the
impression of two little feet.

But she was in a hurry. Lady Celia loved her granddaughter, of course, but could it be that she loved her scones more?

'Sylvia has run off somewhere, but I'm not wasting another minute. My morning tea is getting cold.'

She peered into the mirror again. 'There's nothing in here, not even my reflection. That child is a menace!'

And with that, Lady Celia turned and waddled back down the stairs.

CHAPTER 6

Boubles-land

Not very far away, Mr Badger was making his own way down another flight of stairs, towards a small red boat.

'Hello there, Mr Badger!' called a friendly voice from across the narrow strip of water.

I feel like I know that voice, but who might it be? wondered Mr Badger, setting off across the moat.

As he drew nearer to the castle, Mr Badger saw a ticket booth. In it sat a familiar figure wearing a brightly coloured shirt with palm trees on it.

It was Sir Cecil Smothers-Carruthers.

'You'll not be needing a ticket,' said Sir Cecil. 'You're here as my guest.'

Mr Badger had a number of excellent qualities, and the two that stood out most were his good manners and his calmness in every situation. No matter how difficult or strange things got, Mr Badger always kept a cool head, and Sir Cecil valued him for that. Mr Badger's quick thinking had helped Sir Cecil out of many tricky situations.

'Why thank you, Sir Cecil. I'm thrilled to be here,' said Mr Badger. He wasn't exactly sure *where* he was, but it seemed rude to ask.

Mr Badger felt very welcome.

'Welcome to Boubles-land –
pronounced *Boublay-land*,' said Sir Cecil.
'I've been dropping in here for as long
as I can remember. Not everyone is
able to come here, though, and in any
case I expect not everyone would want
to visit. Some people might not even
believe that such a place could exist.'

Mr Badger was amazed that Boubles-
land could have gone unnoticed by
both guests and hotel staff. But he felt
it might be impolite to ask questions so
early in his visit, so he decided to just
enjoy himself – in fact, to treat this like
a lovely short holiday by the seaside.

CHAPTER 7

A Grand Tour

No sooner had Sir Cecil announced it was time for a tour than Mr Badger heard the *boom, boom, boom* of heavy footsteps.

'Aha!' said Sir Cecil. 'Mr Badger, I'd like you to meet my very close friend, Algernon.'

'How do you do,' said a deep, husky voice as a familiar figure extended a very large hand.

It was none other than Algernon the ape. 'A pleasure to meet you, Algernon,' Mr Badger said warmly, shaking the outstretched hand and noting Algernon and Sir Cecil's matching shirts.

'How do you do,' came a voice from above.

'Now, let us show you the castle,' said Sir Cecil.

'Wonderful,' Mr Badger said, thinking how nice it was for *him* to be treated like a special guest for a change.

Sir Cecil beckoned for Mr Badger
to follow them inside the castle.
Algernon led the way, opening huge
wooden doors into a magnificent
lofty hall.

Inside the hall was an enormous
funfair. From the ceiling, a giant slide
descended in swirling loops, surrounded
by every imaginable ride: bouncy ones
that moved up and down, and whirly
ones which went round and round.
There was even a beautiful carousel.

'It has twenty-seven golden horses
and two chariots,' said Sir Cecil
excitedly. 'And I've tried them all.'

'And a dragon and wooden ostrich,'
added Algernon.

'We often call in here after a safari,' said Sir Cecil. 'This is my personal playground. It brings back memories of my childhood, Mr Badger.'

Even though Mr Badger had long ago left behind his own childhood, he sometimes felt that he carried parts of it within him – memories both good and bad. And there was something about Boubles-land that stirred them back to life for him, too.

Mr Badger tried the slide, the swing
and the wonderful whirligig. He had
a ride on a golden horse while Algernon
relaxed in the chariot and Sir Cecil sat
on the back of the wooden ostrich.

After all this excitement, Sir Cecil laid a cloth on a picnic table while Algernon unpacked lunch for three. There were sandwiches, tea and a big banana cake.

'He's certainly one for the banana cake. Bakes them himself,' said Sir Cecil, waving at Algernon with one hand while passing Mr Badger a napkin with the other.

While this merry little group ate their lunch, unseen eyes followed their every bite. But not even Algernon saw the darting hand that grabbed the last piece of his banana cake and quietly poured tea into a spare cup.

CHAPTER 8

Danger Lurks

After they had cleaned away the crumbs, the three friends returned to the moat. Algernon fetched the little boat again and they all hopped in, bobbing along on the water.

'Not afraid of the dark, I hope?' whispered Sir Cecil, switching on his torch. 'I don't believe in wasting electricity, and anyhow, a bit of dark and the odd surprise can make a journey more exciting.'

While Sir Cecil and Mr Badger
sat up the front, Algernon confidently
took charge and steered the boat into
a channel beneath the castle.

'I come here to relax,' said Sir Cecil,
flashing his torch about. 'Explore, sit
and think, or just chat with Algernon.'

As the boat gently moved through the tunnel, Mr Badger admired a series of different displays. They were lit by tiny lights as well as the occasional beam from Sir Cecil's torch.

'Made them myself,' said Sir Cecil proudly, pointing at the various scenes. 'All plaster, wood and papier-mâché. Frighteningly realistic, aren't they?'

Mr Badger noted that each scene
was like a shop-window display: here,
some reindeer caught in mid-leap; there,
a scene in the Swiss Alps with papier-
mâché mountain climbers. Yet another
scene showed some ancient cavemen.
There were some cavewomen, too.
And nearby was a family of sweet little
gnomes sitting outside their toadstool
house.

271

'Quite a mixture,' he said, impressed.

Even though Mr Badger appreciated the gnomes outside their toadstool house, one gnome with a curled lip left him feeling uneasy – and his instincts were proven correct for, sure enough, as they passed, this particular gnome leapt off the toadstool and hissed, then bared its razor-sharp teeth.

While Mr Badger was alarmed at first, neither Algernon nor Sir Cecil took any notice, so Mr Badger followed their example and settled back to enjoy the ride. The boat continued to move gently on its journey along the channel beneath the castle.

Suddenly, out of the darkness leapt a hideous creature with long webbed feet. Green and slimy scales covered its body, and devil-like horns protruded from an awful head. It snarled, revealing rotten yellow fangs.

'Take no notice,' said Sir Cecil. 'I'm sure its bark is worse than its bite.'

Raising his eyebrows, Mr Badger did as requested and looked the other way.

It was a horrifying sight.

His eyes had barely adjusted to the
dark again when, without any warning,
an even more terrifying sight presented
itself right in front of him. It was
a ghost, with eyes glowing red and a
body white and shimmering. Emitting
a horrible howl, it lurched towards
Sir Cecil and a startled Mr Badger.

'Oh, do move along, please,' requested Sir Cecil, brushing past the phantom. 'Now I must show you my sailing ship, Mr Badger.'

They continued on their tour for quite some time in peace after that, unaware that they were to be disturbed once more...

CHAPTER 9

More Surprises

The little boat stopped alongside a magnificent galleon. While Algernon kept one foot in the tiny boat and the other on the deck of the galleon, he hoisted Sir Cecil and Mr Badger up with a swing of his very long arm.

Sir Cecil was proudly showing Mr Badger over his ship when a blood-curdling scream came from high up in the main mast. Down dropped a pirate, brandishing a cutlass.

'Good heavens!' said Mr Badger. He had never met a pirate before.

It was a small but nasty pirate.

This was a very short pirate, but a pirate nonetheless, with disgusting teeth and greasy hair pulled back into an untidy pigtail. One eye – no doubt lost in a sword fight – was covered with a patch.

On the pirate's head sat a big black hat with skull and crossbones, just like Mr Badger had seen in his pirate books, while in the middle of a nasty, mean face sat a cruel and evil smile.

'Move it, measly scum!' said the rude pirate, waving the cutlass menacingly. 'I'll have you walking the plank, down, down deep into the shark-infested waters below.'

It was a long way down, and Mr Badger couldn't swim.

Mr Badger looked over the side.
It certainly was a long way down, and
he was scared of heights.

'I beg your pardon,' replied Sir Cecil
Smothers-Carruthers, as cool as a
cucumber. 'We'll be doing no such thing.'

Mr Badger wondered if their luck had run out, for this pushy pirate seemed scarier than the web-footed monster, the red-eyed phantom and the nasty fanged gnome all put together.

What a day – and where will it end? he thought, noting again that it was quite a drop to the murky waters below, and remembering with a shudder that he couldn't swim.

'Step aside, you beastly brute,' demanded Sir Cecil bravely.

But the pushy pirate continued to wave the cutlass, edging them along the wobbling plank. Mr Badger tried not to look down.

Suddenly, with a giant leap, Algernon jumped into the air and landed back on the plank with an almighty thud, shaking the weapon from the pirate's hand.

Mr Badger was bounced way uuuuuuuuup into the air. *Oh dear*, he thought, closing his eyes, waiting for the splash. He thought of darling

daughter Berenice and baby
Badger's bedtime stories...and muffins
and hot chocolate with Mrs Badger!
Would he ever see them again?

However, instead of plunging down
into the water, Algernon caught
Mr Badger and tossed him in a giant
arc across the sky...

...bouncing him right through the magic mirror, away from Boubles-land, and safely out of harm's way.

It was amazing. Mr Badger was back where he'd begun.

Lady Celia was on the warpath.

At precisely the moment Mr Badger landed on his feet at the top of the stairs, Lady Celia Smothers-Carruthers came puffing along the corridor.

'You haven't seen my granddaughter, have you, Badger?' she demanded. 'Sylvia's been gone quite some time, the mischievous little monster. And that tour group from Australia has, as I expected, eaten all the scones!'

Lady Celia was beside herself.

CHAPTER 10

Back at the
Boubles Grand Hotel

That afternoon, in spite of his extraordinary adventure, Mr Badger was ready as usual to meet and greet the visitors pouring into the foyer of the Boubles Grand Hotel. Naturally the guests included Lady Celia and, yes, Sylvia Smothers-Carruthers – who had mysteriously reappeared – for afternoon tea in the lounge.

'How do you do, Lady Celia?' inquired Mr Badger, polite as ever.

'Fine, Badger,' came a rather rude
reply as Lady Celia brushed past.

'Good afternoon, Miss Sylvia,' said
Mr Badger to Lady Celia's grumpy
granddaughter, who turned up her nose
and looked away.

He could tell that Lady Celia had
a lot on her mind: little Sylvia was
in one of her moods, tugging on her
grandmother's arm and pointing.

'No, we are *not* going to the top of the stairs,' snapped Lady Celia. 'There is no such thing as a magic mirror! It's teatime, and I've ordered a special fig jam for my scones.' With that, she dragged Sylvia into the lounge.

For a moment, Mr Badger was more than a little stunned.

He walked up the stairs and gazed at the mirror.

'Good afternoon, Mr Badger,' said a voice from behind. 'I see you're admiring my mirror.'

'Good afternoon, Mr Badger.'

Mr Badger turned to find Sir Cecil Smothers-Carruthers smiling at him.

'My wife wants me to throw it out,' said Sir Cecil, 'but I know for a fact that *some* people appreciate it. And, Mr Badger, I've a feeling that you may well be one of them.'

Mr Badger nodded in agreement as he accompanied Sir Cecil down the stairs towards the dining room, where Sir Cecil was to join Lady Celia and little Sylvia for tea and scones.

'Isn't life full of surprises!' said Sir Cecil with a chuckle, waving his walking stick merrily at Algernon, who was standing in his glass case in the foyer wearing a brightly coloured shirt with palm trees on it.

'Yes, indeed it is,' replied Mr Badger. 'And, Sir Cecil, I can truly say that many of them are right here in the Boubles Grand Hotel.'

'So true,' said Sir Cecil with a wink. 'So true.'

CHAPTER 11

A Tale to Tell

As if through a fog, Mr Badger heard, very faintly at first, another voice. A warm and familiar voice. It seemed to come from far away, and yet it sounded strangely close...

'I really think it's time for bed, dear.'

Mr Badger blinked and opened his eyes. He was sitting in a chair with a book on his lap. Next to him were two little badgers snuggled in bed, darling daughter Berenice and baby Badger, too, wrapped in each other's arms.

'I really think it's time for bed, dear,'
said a familiar voice.

'You've been asleep for ever so long,'
said Mrs Badger, 'but I didn't have the
heart to wake you. In fact, you nodded
off very soon after you began reading
your story.'

'Ah,' said Mr Badger, sipping a cup of hot chocolate. 'I am very tired, but there's something I just *have* to tell you. You might not believe your ears ... but the strangest thing happened to me today at the Boubles Grand Hotel!'

'Oh really?' smiled Mrs Badger. 'I can't wait to hear all about it.'

The End

A Little Bit about the Author

Mr Badger is unlike the rest of Leigh Hobbs' characters, as he lives in a real city – London.

Many years ago, Leigh lived there too. Every day he would catch a bright-red double-decker bus into the centre of London, hop off at Trafalgar Square, and set off in a different direction.

Occasionally, Leigh would walk past a place quite similar to the Boubles Grand Hotel. Sometimes he even put on a tie and went in for afternoon tea.

Alas, these must have been the very days when Mr Badger was busy doing other things rather than helping serve tea and scones with jam, for he and Leigh never met…back then.